Enjoy Reading Your Book
Look for the VERBS!!

Happy Birthday Austin

from — Gramma with love.

Nobody Rides the Unicorn

Nobody Rides
the Unicorn

story by

A D R I A N M I T C H E L L

illustrated by

S T E P H E N L A M B E R T

ARTHUR A. LEVINE BOOKS

An Imprint of Scholastic Press

New York

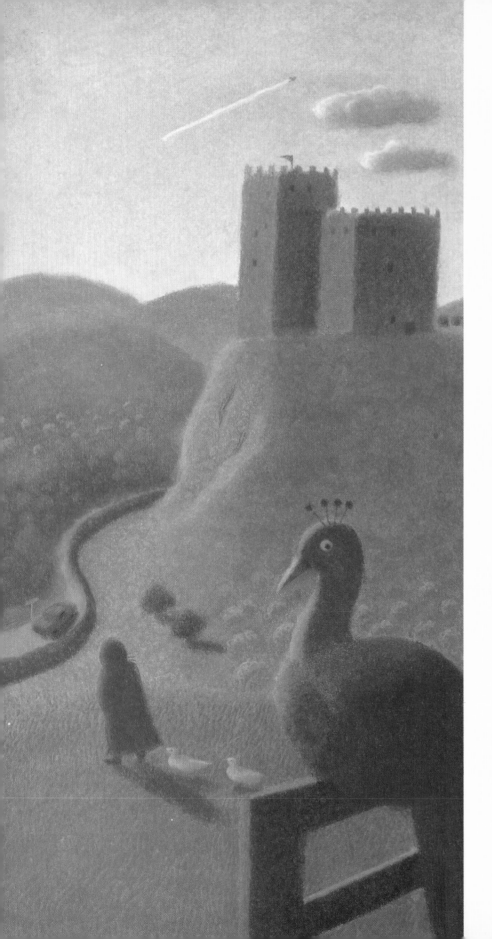

I n the faraway land of Joppardy
there was once a king who was full
of fear. He was afraid of everybody
in the world. He was sure they were
plotting to put poison in his wine or
in his food.

So the king called the most cunning
man in Joppardy, a man named Doctor
Slythe.

"There is only one sure way to avoid being poisoned," said Doctor Slythe. "You must drink from a goblet made of a unicorn's horn. And you must eat with a knife, fork, and spoon made from a unicorn's horn."

"But how can I catch a unicorn?" asked the king. "Such a beast is too fierce and fast for my hounds."

Doctor Slythe whispered in his ear: "The unicorn can only be trapped by a quiet young girl with a gentle voice."

"So—find me that girl!" bellowed the king.

Doctor Slythe sent for Zoe, the beggar girl. She was the quietest,
gentlest girl in all of Joppardy. But she lived alone. She was nobody's child.

Zoe was brought before the king. Doctor Slythe told her, "We will take you into the deep forest and you will sit alone, singing sweetly and softly. After a while, perhaps, a unicorn will appear and come lay his head in your lap."

Zoe was very excited and scared, but she wanted to see the unicorn. So she went with the king and the doctor into the deep forest and sat alone, waiting under a silver birch tree. After a while she began to sing, very sweetly and softly, a song that she had learned in her dreams:

HIS COAT IS LIKE SNOWFLAKES
WOVEN WITH SILK.
WHEN HE GOES GALLOPING
HE FLOWS LIKE MILK.

HIS LIFE IS ALL GENTLE
AND HIS HEART IS BOLD.
HIS HORN IS MAGICAL,
LIVING GOLD.

NOBODY RIDES THE UNICORN.
HE GRAZES UNDER A SECRET SUN.
HIS UNDERSTANDING IS SO GREAT
THAT HE FORGIVES US, EVERY ONE.

NOBODY RIDES THE UNICORN.
HIS MIND IS PEACEFUL AS THE GRASS.
HE IS THE LOVELIEST ONE OF ALL
AND HE LIVES BEHIND THE WATERFALL.

While she sang, Zoe looked down at the flowers around her feet. And when she looked up, there was the unicorn.

His dark, golden eyes gazed into hers. He snuffled and stamped his hooves on the earth. Then he lay down and put his head in her lap.

She said, "Good unicorn, good unicorn," and tickled him under the chin. His breathing was warm and musical, and before long he closed his eyes in sleep.

Suddenly the air was torn by trumpets. Out of the forest ran a hundred huntsmen. There was a terrible struggle, and the unicorn was wounded seven times by spears and hounds.

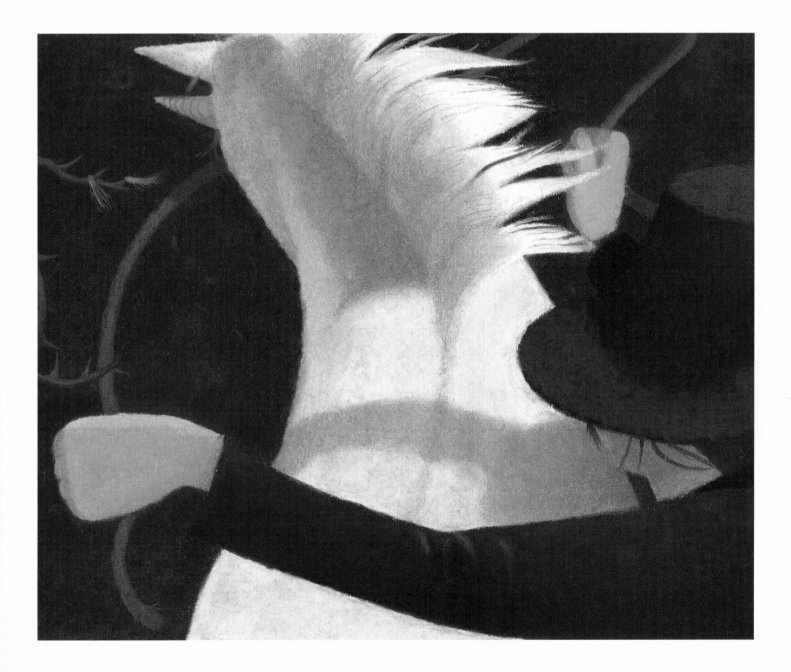

But he fought on until Doctor Slythe crept up behind him and threw a magical, golden bridle around his neck.

Then the unicorn stood still and allowed himself to be led out of the forest and down the road by the river and through the streets of the city and into the garden of the royal palace.

There the unicorn was pushed into a paddock surrounded by a strong fence. And the unicorn was chained to a tree.

ow Zoe was very angry,
he had been used to trick
unicorn and make him a
oner. And she knew that
wrong.
hen she heard the king
the doctor planning to kill
unicorn and make a goblet
knives and forks and
ons out of its beautiful horn,
was angry enough to burst.
t Zoe was clever. She hid
anger, and, in the middle
he night, she crept into the
ens of the royal palace,
ned the wounds of the
corn, and set him free.

The unicorn lowered his head once to her and gazed into her eyes. Then he neighed once and galloped off down the streets of the sleeping city, along the road beside the river, and into the depths of the forest.

When the king heard that the unicorn had escaped and that Zoe had set him free, he shouted at her, "You shall be banished! I order that from this day on, no one in Joppardy shall speak to this little nobody!"

Zoe was in disgrace and she had nowhere to go. She thought of the unicorn, but where could she find him? Then she remembered those lines from her dream song:

HE IS THE LOVELIEST ONE OF ALL
AND HE LIVES BEHIND THE WATERFALL.

Zoe left the city and followed the road beside the river. A full moon changed the water to silver. She followed its shining path as it wound its way through the forest toward the bright mountains.

Suddenly she was face to face
with the waterfall, huge and
powerful. Zoe started to climb it
but the water poured down,
strong and icy, and the cold hur
her hands so much that she crie

Then, without warning, Zoe
lost her footing and found herse
falling through the waterfall and
into a cave. There might have
been snakes. There might have
been bears. But Zoe thought onl
of the unicorn as she scrambled
through the cave, toward a spec
of light that became bigger and
bigger, till she came out the
other side.

Zoe looked down into the secret valley of the unicorns. There she saw the unicorns dancing together slowly in the moonlight.

She sat down to watch them and was so happy that she began to sing. Zoe's unicorn turned away from the dancing and trotted over to her.

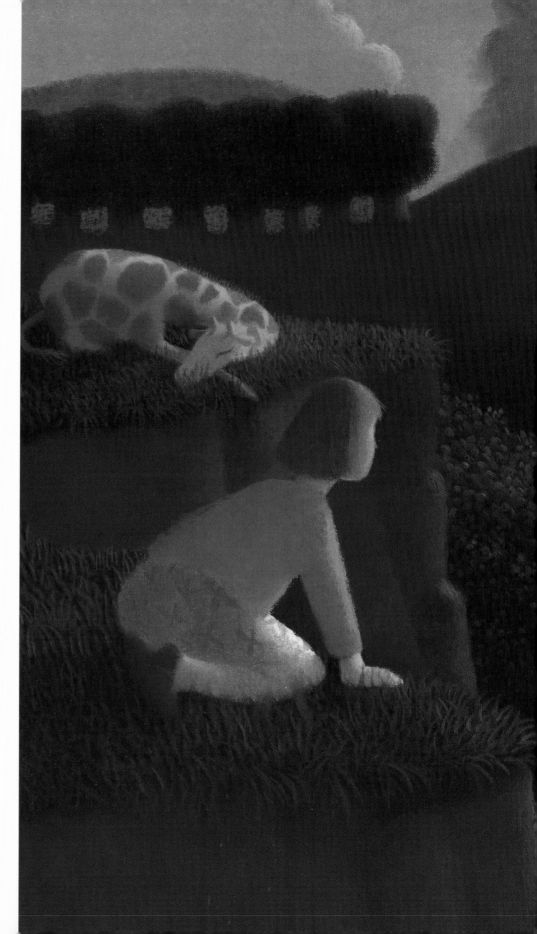

His dark, golden eyes gazed into hers. He snuffled and stamped his hooves on the earth. Then he lay down and put his head in her lap. She said, "Good unicorn, good unicorn," and she tickled him under the chin. Then she sang her dream song, sweetly and softly.

At the end of Zoe's song, the unicorn's dark, golden eyes spoke to her, saying, "Tell me, my kind friend, who are you?"

Zoe said, "Me, I'm nobody."

"Climb on my back, kind Nobody," said the unicorn with his eyes. "For Nobody rides the unicorn."

So Zoe climbed on to his back and held on to his mane. And together they trotted down into the secret valley of the unicorns.

WITH LOVE TO NATASHA, CHARLOTTE, CAITLIN, ZOE, ARTHUR, AND LOLA

—MY GRANDCHILDREN.

A. M.

Text copyright © 1999 by Adrian Mitchell
Illustrations copyright © 1999 by Stephen Lambert
All rights reserved. Published by Scholastic Press, a division of Scholastic Inc.,
Publishers since 1920, 555 Broadway, New York, NY 10012 by arrangement with
Transworld Publishers Ltd. SCHOLASTIC, SCHOLASTIC PRESS, ARTHUR A. LEVINE BOOKS
and associated logos are trademarks and/or registered trademarks of Scholastic Inc.

Library of Congress Cataloging-in-Publication Data

Mitchell, Adrian.
Nobody rides the unicorn / by Adrian Mitchell; illustrated by Stephen Lambert.
p.   cm.
Summary: Having been used by the king to trick a unicorn
into imprisonment, Zoe decides to set him free again.
ISBN 0-439-11204-4
[1. Unicorn—Fiction.]
I. Lambert, Stephen, 1964–, ill. II. Title.
PZ7.M685No   2000
[E]—dc21   99-27374

10 9 8 7 6 5 4 3 2 1   0/0 01 02 03 04
Printed in Singapore
First American edition, April 2000